Dragos Cuelebre is no longer the only dragon.

Dragos's son Liam Cuelebre (a.k.a. Peanut) is springing into existence, reminiscent of the first of the Elder Races who were born at the beginning of the world. At just six months of age, he has already grown to the size of a large five-year-old boy. He can read, write in complete sentences, and his math skills are off the chart.

A white dragon in his Wyr form, Liam also holds more Power than almost anyone else. In an effort to give him a taste of normality, no matter how fleeting, his parents Pia and Dragos enroll him in first grade.

They hope school will help teach Liam how to relate to others, a vital skill that will help him control his growing Power. But school has a surprising number of pitfalls, and relating to others can be a tricky business.

When a classmate is threatened, Liam must quickly learn self-control, how to rein in his instincts, and govern his temper, because there's no doubt about it—he is fast becoming one of the most dangerous creatures in all of the Elder Races.

Peanut Goes To School

To School

Thea Harrison

*To my copyeditor, Luann, who
makes every story better.*

Chapter One

THE TRICKY THING about using a cloaking spell is that cloaking spells are tricky.

Liam snickered to himself as he tiptoed around the patio furniture and changed into his dragon form. His dragon had grown to the size of an adult lion, and he had to be careful not to knock over the furniture as he shapeshifted.

He also managed to hold on to his cloaking spell, which was a big fat win. Dad had said Liam's cloaking ability was one of the best he'd ever seen, although it was difficult to stay hidden while changing forms.

But since his dad could do it, Liam felt sure he would be able to do it also. Eventually. Sometimes. If he kept practicing, pretty soon he should be able to stay cloaked all the time if he needed to.

Liam was playing his favorite game, Spy Wyr, which he had totally made up himself. When he grew up, he was going to be a secret sentinel. Uncle Graydon would send him out on missions, and when he returned after saving somebody, or maybe even after saving everybody, Mom and Dad would be really proud of him.

Of course, because it was undercover, Dad would have to give him medals in secret. Sometimes they might be silver and bronze ones, or when he did something amazing, they might be gold. Or maybe when he did something really outstanding, Dad would give him a sparkly medal with diamonds on it. Then Liam would have to find a super-secret place to hide them.

His dragon side liked the sound of that. It made him feel growly and fine.

By day, Liam would be, oh, maybe a basketball player. Basketball players traveled a lot, so it would be a good cover, and besides, it would be fun to play ball all the time, so that would be a big fat win.

Hi, my name is Cuelebre, Liam Cuelebre. My code name is Double Oh Peanut, but you can call me Rock Star for short.

Snickering again, he started climbing the house. It was a big house and there was a lot of brick on the outside. If he had been in his human form, he wouldn't have been able to climb it, but in his dragon form, he could get a good grip by digging the tips of his talons into the brick.

One of his favorite things to do was sit on the roof and look around. Hugh said it was his perching instinct. Dad said he would have to get the roof reinforced, because Liam was going to get a lot bigger before he finished growing.

It was mid-August, but the day was nice and cool for a change, so lots of windows were open. And even though it was Sunday, there were always plenty of people about. Hesitating as he clung to the side of the house, he tried to decide who he wanted to spy on next.

Mom and Dad were hanging out in their rooms. . . . They had been relaxing a lot since Dad got hurt the month before.

If Liam could sneak past Dad's superpowers of detection, he was pretty sure he could sneak past anything. That might go a long way toward convincing Uncle Graydon to hire him for spy missions when he got bigger.

Once the idea occurred to him, he couldn't shake it loose. Giving into temptation, he climbed sideways to the end of the house, around the corner and up to Mom and Dad's balcony. It was a lot more work than he had anticipated, so he got tired, and he was glad to reach the point where he could cling to a support beam on the underside of the balcony.

From overhead came the sound of quiet rustling and the creak of furniture. Mom and Dad were outside on the balcony. They sounded like they might be cuddling.

Liam loved to cuddle with them and sprawl in a big heap to watch movies or football games. As he thought of joining them, he started to lose interest in playing Spy Wyr.

Then Mom said in a quiet voice, "I feel like it's all my fault."

"You know that's not true," Dad replied. "He was growing quickly before you said anything to him."

Liam started to get a hot, tight feeling somewhere in his middle. Were they talking about him?

"I know, but I'd give almost anything to turn back time and take back what I said."

Liam's wings and tail drooped. He knew exactly what she was talking about. They *were* talking about him, and Mom sounded really sad.

Last month, when Dad had gotten hurt so bad, Mom had said to Liam, *You need to be a big soldier now.*

And Liam had thought, I can do that.

He had *pushed* to get bigger, because Mom needed him to be strong.

Getting bigger wasn't hard. It was kind of like shapeshifting, and his dragon form wanted him to be big anyway. He could feel it inside, straining to encompass all of his Power. And, as Dad had said, he was growing awfully fast anyway. But for some reason, when he had gone through that growth spurt, it had hurt Mom, and the last thing in the world Liam wanted to do was hurt her.

For the first time ever, he thought, Am I bad?

Asking that question made the hot, tight feeling in his middle worse.

"I can't believe I'm going to take him to school in the morning," Mom said. "Even though he's taller than most first graders, he's only six months old."

"We've talked about this," Dad said. "We agreed that he needed school."

"I know and I was even the one who argued for that, but I have to ask—are we going about this the right way? He's already far past what a normal first grader knows anyway. He's read through a third of our library, he writes in complete sentences, and he's been learning high-school algebra from Hugh." She muttered, "*I* don't even remember how to do high-school algebra."

"Never mind the academics," Dad said. "You were right. He needs the socialization. The only people he interacts with are adults. He has to learn to relate to other children too, while he's still a child."

"I agree," Mom told him. "I'm just fretting. Dragos, he's so innocent."

"I know, but that innocent boy is also a dangerous predator. He can already take down animals that are more than twice the size of his Wyr form."

It was only one cow, Liam thought. He hadn't thought it was that big of a deal.

Dad was still talking. "When he killed those cows, Hugh said he went into a complete frenzy."

Okay, Liam might have forgotten about the other cows. His snout itched, and he rubbed it on one forearm.

"He needs to learn how to control himself," Dad said. "And for that, he needs to develop social ties. Relationships will be the only real check on him when he grows to his full size. He has to care enough about other people so that he controls himself, for their sake."

Mom whispered, "Like you?"

"Yes," said Dad. "Exactly like me."

They fell silent. Liam suspected they might be kissing, which they liked to do a lot.

From around the corner, in the direction of the kitchen, Hugh called out, "Liam, come on in. It's time for lunch."

He heaved a sigh. He didn't want to leave. He wanted to listen to Mom and Dad talk until they said something that made everything better. He wanted that hot, tight feeling to go away.

"Liam!" Hugh shouted. "Don't make me come after you, buddy."

He could tell Hugh was too cheerful to be mad. Hugh almost never got mad, but Liam also didn't want Hugh to find out where he was, because then Mom and Dad would find out too, and what was the point of spying if you couldn't keep it a secret?

Releasing his hold on the support beam, he let himself fall. Like a cat, he twisted in midair so that he landed in a crouch, right side up. Trudging around the corner of the house, he shapeshifted back into a human boy and went inside for lunch.

The rest of the day seemed to go on forever. Desultorily, Liam played Spy Wyr some more, but his heart wasn't in it.

He was starting to feel nervous about school. What if the other kids didn't like him? How was he supposed to learn to socialize, if that happened? From the way Dad was talking, it sounded pretty important.

And besides, what if he didn't make any friends?

For supper, Mom cooked his favorite meal, spaghetti with meatballs, and Liam, Mom and Dad ate together in the breakfast nook off the kitchen. Mom had meatballs with her spaghetti too, but hers were the fake kind. Liam wasn't like Dad about food—even though he liked real meat a lot better, he liked fake meatballs just fine too.

For some reason, tonight his spaghetti noodles were hard to swallow, and he pushed the meatballs around his plate, until Mom frowned and asked, "Are you feeling all right, sweetheart?"

He wasn't sure. All his feelings were tangled up in a knot, and he didn't know how to untangle them, or how to answer her. So, he shrugged and said, "Sure."

She looked at him for a long, thoughtful moment. "I've never seen you without an appetite."

After thinking about it for a moment, he shrugged again. "Me neither."

Both Mom and Dad laughed, and then it was Dad's turn to study him. Dad's keen, gold gaze seemed to see everything, and Liam squirmed in his seat. But all Dad said was, "Maybe you'll be hungry later, or in the morning."

"Sure, maybe," he mumbled, fiddling with his napkin.

"Why don't you go upstairs and take your bath?" Mom suggested. "I'll be up soon to tuck you into bed."

Liam looked outside. It was still plenty light outside, but Mom had already talked to him about how he would have to go to bed earlier on school nights. At the time, he hadn't minded, but now it kind of sucked.

"Do I have to?" he asked. "It's so early, and I'm not tired."

"Yes, you have to." She smiled at him. Mom's smiles were the most beautiful thing in the world, and they almost always made things better. They almost even made an early bedtime okay, but not quite.

He thought about arguing, but he could tell by the calm look on their faces that Mom and Dad were going to team up on this one.

He heaved an aggrieved sigh. "Okay, fine."

As he slid out of his seat and stood, Dad swept a large arm around him and pulled him in for a hug. Liam leaned against him. Dad was so big and strong that when Liam leaned on him, it was hard to be afraid.

The problem was, he couldn't lean on Dad forever. He had to go to school by himself.

As he straightened, Dad kissed him on the forehead. Mom said, "See you in a few minutes."

Upstairs, he gave his bath toys some consideration, but he didn't feel like playing anymore, so he took a shower instead. After drying his hair and putting on some underpants, he went to his closet and pulled out a pair of tan khaki shorts and a yellow and blue plaid shirt. The shirt had a collar, and it buttoned down the front. The yellow and blue colors reminded him of the sky.

It was his favorite outfit. He slipped on the khakis and shrugged into the shirt. He was just beginning to button it when Mom walked into his room.

Her eyebrows went up. "What are you doing?"

"I'm getting dressed for school," he told her.

The beginnings of a confused smile tugged at the corner of her mouth. "Sweetie, you do realize you don't go to school until the morning."

He gave her a serious look. "I know that."

"So why are you putting on your school clothes?"

He toed the carpet with one bare foot. "I don't want to be late. I thought it might be better if I got dressed now."

Her smile faded, and she gave him a completely serious look back. Then she went to sit in the rocking chair where she would rock him when he was a baby. Since he had gotten so big, they had taken out the crib and put in a real bed, but they had kept the rocking chair.

Actually, he might still like it when Mom rocked him in the chair. Sometimes. As long as she didn't tell anyone, and she had promised she wouldn't.

Mom had to move Bunny out of the way. Leaning forward, she rested her elbows on her knees as she held the stuffed toy in both hands.

"Tomorrow's a pretty big deal," she said. "I understand if you need to wear your school clothes tonight, just to be sure. But what if I cross-my-heart promise that you will have plenty of time to get dressed in the morning, and eat a good breakfast too, and you will still be on time for school? Does that help?"

Lifting one shoulder, he admitted, "It might."

"You can still sleep in your school clothes if you want, but if you do, they'll wrinkle, and you might not want to wear them in the morning."

He frowned. He wanted to wear this outfit tomorrow, not something else. "Okay, I'll put on my pjs."

"I think that's a smart choice. You'll be a lot more comfortable." As he changed into his Superman pajamas, she petted Bunny between its floppy ears. "Can you tell me why you're so nervous about school?"

He gave it some thought.

He couldn't ask her if he was bad, because what if he was? And what if other people could tell that he was?

What if Mom didn't know he was bad until he asked her, but then she found out? The hot, tight feeling came back. He had never thought of loss before Dad got hurt, but now he had. And he couldn't lose his mom. He just couldn't.

When she spoke again, her voice was quieter, gentler. "Liam, are you okay?"

Ducking his head, he mumbled, "I dunno."

"Would you like to rock with me for a few minutes?"

He nodded. She sat back in the rocking chair, and as he climbed in her lap, she wrapped her arms around him. He put his head on her shoulder, and she rocked him. After a while, she handed Bunny to him, and he smiled as he looked down at the toy. He was much too big for it now, but he still liked having it around.

"Look at those legs of yours," she said. "Look at those big feet."

She poked him in the thigh until he squirmed and laughed. They took a moment to look at his legs. They were too long, and his feet dangled almost to the floor, but he didn't care.

"Pretty soon you're going to be too big to ride on my back," she said softly.

A pang struck. He loved, loved, loved her Wyr form, and he was never happier than when she took him for rides in the forest that summer.

He whispered, "I can't stop growing."

Immediately, she clasped him in a tight hold. "Of course you can't," she told him in a strong voice. "Nor should you. We're just going to have to flip things around. When you get big enough, I'm going to ride on *your* back instead."

He started to smile. "Really?"

"Absolutely. And I will love it every bit as much. Pinky swear." She pressed her lips to his forehead. "There aren't any words big enough to tell you how much I love you."

Well, space was pretty big. In fact, it was the biggest thing he knew of. He told her, "I love you bigger than space."

Tilting her head, she smiled into his eyes. "How perfect. I love you bigger than space too."

They rocked until gradually the tight, hot feeling eased, and he felt better. When she suggested he climb into bed, he didn't argue, and after she tucked the covers around him, she gave him one last kiss and turned the lights out as she left.

Rolling over, Liam fell asleep almost immediately and dreamed of how delicious the warm, fresh blood from the cows had tasted as it gushed down his throat.

Chapter Two

MOM KEPT HER promise and woke him early enough so he could put on his favorite clothes and sit down to a big breakfast of scrambled eggs and steak with Dad.

Dad was dressed for work too, but he didn't wear suits as often in their new home as he did when he was in the city. Today he wore jeans and a black T-shirt, although he had a stack of business papers with him at the table.

Liam bounced in his chair and waved his fork around as he talked around mouthfuls of food. Sometimes he pretended to conduct an invisible orchestra. The third time he asked what time it was, Dad got up from the table and left the kitchen area.

After a few moments he returned with a portable alarm clock, which he set directly in front of Liam's plate with such a look at Liam that he had to giggle. Out of the corner of his eye, he could see that Mom was laughing quietly too.

"Sorry, not sorry," Liam said. He had picked that one up off the Internet.

"So I can see," said Dad, with one black eyebrow raised.

Mom went to the kitchen for more coffee, which was when Dad turned to look him in the eye. All the humor was gone from his face, and it made Liam sober too.

"You're going to be stronger than anyone else today, including the teachers," said Dad in a quiet way that said he meant business. "Hugh and a few other guards will be nearby to keep an eye on things, but they won't be on school grounds. I want you to promise me you'll watch your temper, and you'll do as your teacher says."

"Yessir," said Liam. He sat up straight.

Dad gave him a smile. "Good boy."

But what if he wasn't? What if he wasn't a good boy?

The hot, tight feeling returned, and he had to put down his fork. He asked, "May I be excused?"

Dad's gaze went to the food that Liam had left on his plate, but he didn't say anything about it. Instead, he said, "Sure. Go brush your teeth and get your backpack."

Liam's new backpack was full of everything on his school list, like glue, scissors, and crayons. He dashed off to do as he was told, and all too soon, Mom, Eva and he piled into one of the SUVs and headed for school.

The trip seemed to take forever, but all of a sudden, Eva made a right turn, and he realized they were pulling into the school parking lot.

He stared curiously at the large school playground, which was located behind a tall, chain link fence. Big trees offered lots of shade, and there were two jungle gyms, along with a swing set.

He watched as Mom slipped on a baseball cap and

dark sunglasses. She wore the cap and glasses a lot when they went out. She called it her incognito look. Turning to him, she gave him a bright smile. "Are you ready?"

No. "Yes!"

"Okay, let's go."

As they climbed out of the vehicle, he realized that other parents and kids were going into the school too. Most were either human or Wyr, but he also noticed one girl who looked Dark Fae. Her black hair had been cut into a bob at her chin, and her pointed ears peeked through the shining cap. Like Liam, she was taller than a lot of the other kids, and her large gray eyes darted everywhere.

Mom offered her hand, and he took it. She switched to telepathy. *Don't forget, you're registered as Liam Giovanni, not Liam Cuelebre. The principal knows who you are, but nobody else does.*

I didn't forget, he told her. He liked using Mom's maiden name. It made him feel like he was undercover.

She pulled her sunglasses down her nose to look at him over the top of the rim. *You have so much Power, sweetie. . . . Make sure to keep your cloaking tight around your body, okay? Otherwise you might make someone nervous.*

Okay, he said.

What about your cell phone? Do you have it with you?

Yeah. He patted the pocket of his shorts where the phone rested.

Who do you get if you rapid-dial number one?

He looked up at her. *You.*

That's right. Who is number two?

Dad. He kept staring at the Dark Fae girl when she wasn't looking in their direction. He liked how she looked. She looked sassy.

And number three?

Hugh.

Her fingers tightened on his. *Remember to dial Hugh first, if you need somebody right away, because he'll be just outside the school grounds.*

I won't forget, he told her.

"You're going to have a great day, I just know it," Mom said out loud. Her voice sounded kind of clogged up, like she might be getting a cold. "It's hard to believe that only last year you really were the size of a peanut."

He said, out of the corner of his mouth, "Mom, you promised you weren't going to call me that in public anymore."

"Right! Sorry, sweetheart."

As they reached the doors, he turned to her. "I remember how to get to my classroom. It's okay, you can go home now."

"Sounds good. I'll meet you right here after school." She gave him a smile that looked a bit strange, but he was too busy to question it for long.

"Okay." Pulling his hand free, he hopped to reach up for her kiss.

Usually he was an optimistic guy, and as he darted inside, last night's nervousness became a thing of the past, because Mom was right.

He was going to have a pretty great day.

✧　✧　✧

PIA STARED AFTER Liam as he disappeared into the school building.

Over the last couple of months, his hair had darkened to a honeyed gold, and it wouldn't be long before he stood as tall as her shoulder. Whenever she looked into his eyes, which were the same midnight violet as her own, she caught a glimpse of the Power contained in his tall, young body.

It wasn't the same as Dragos's Power. It didn't boil with quite the same fiery heat. But it was every bit as strong, every bit as vast.

She was so proud of him, and more than a little scared for his future, and she loved him so much, sometimes it squeezed the air right out of her lungs.

And look at how strong and brave he was. He ran into the building without giving her a single backward glance.

Well, that was *good*. Good for him.

As she turned to walk back to the SUV where Eva waited, tears spilled out of her eyes and ran down her cheeks.

Climbing into the passenger seat, she slammed the door and looked straight ahead. "Don't try to talk me out of this. I need to cry it out."

Eva put one dark brown hand on her knee in a gentle pat. "Your baby just went off to school. You go right ahead, and cry all you want to, sugar. Today you get a free pass on anything you want."

Pia nodded, wiped her eyes and stared out the passenger window as Eva drove them back home. The majority of work was finally done on the house, and the focus of construction now centered on the office complex by the lake.

The site where Dragos had been so badly injured last month.

Pia didn't intentionally set out to avoid the area, but for one reason or another, she never went down there after Dragos's accident. She kept telling herself that things would be different once the complex was completed. For now, whenever she stepped through the trees and looked at the scene, all she could remember was the horror and terror she felt when she thought Dragos might have died.

After they parked, Eva gave her a tight hug. "Let me know if you want to talk anything over."

"I will. Thanks." Returning the hug, she went inside to find Dragos.

He was in his office, sitting at his desk and conducting a meeting via the secure telecom system he'd had installed. After days of fierce concentration as he had tried to think of what *the other Dragos*—the Dragos before his accident—would have done, he had finally managed to recreate the password on his computer. As she heard the voices, she recognized two of his sentinels, Graydon and Constantine.

That was how he approached anything to do with his injury and subsequent memory loss. He treated it like a battle and brought all of his formidable attention and tactical skills to the field with the intent to win. Pia found it both exhilarating and exhausting to watch.

Reluctant to interrupt, she hovered in the doorway, but as soon as he caught sight of her, Dragos said to his screen, "We'll have to talk more later. I've got to go now."

"Sure thing." Constantine's voice sounded clearly over the speakers.

Graydon said, "Text me when you're ready to pick this up again."

Then Dragos strode around the corner of his desk, wearing a look of concern on his hard features. He frowned. "You've been crying."

She gave him a twisted smile. "Yeah, I got emotional after I watched Liam go into the building. He didn't want me to come with him, and he ran in without a backward glance, and I was so glad that he was strong and secure enough to do that. . . . Then I cried like a baby all the way home."

He pulled her into his arms, and she went gladly, soaking in the feeling of his fierce energy as it wrapped around her protectively.

She found her favorite spot, the slight hollow of breastbone in the middle of his chest where she could rest her cheek. They stood like that for moment and then she said, "I don't want to be a helicopter parent, but you know, if he keeps growing like this, he's going to be . . . What, like a twenty-eight-year-old when he's actually two? That bends my head, and it makes me worry."

She felt Dragos shaking his head. "Tough as it is to

adjust your thinking, we're never going to be able to judge him by normal standards. He's too much of a prodigy."

"I know, but my own past was so human, I don't understand how he knows the things he knows."

His fingers threaded through her hair. "The first-generation of the Elder Races were all fully formed when they came into being at the birth of the world. Magic has long since settled into balance, but in the beginning, it was nowhere near as defined. It ran hot and wild, and crazy things happened. It's possible the only reason Liam is having any kind of childhood experience at all is because he was conceived, and he didn't form spontaneously as the first generation did."

She thought back to her shock when she first found out she was pregnant. She muttered, "His conception seemed kind of spontaneous to me."

She could hear the smile in Dragos's voice as he continued, "He's also the product of two very rare and magical parents, and the combined Power he has inherited from each of us is quite unique. If he had been conceived at the beginning of the world, he might have sprung into existence fully formed too. As it is, he has to contend with the laws of nature as they are now."

As she listened to him, she calmed. He was always so much warmer than her. She reveled in his body warmth, in the hard strength of his arms resting around her, in all the sensual evidence of his presence. "I love listening to stories about how things were in the beginning. It sounds fascinating."

"It was a dangerous and unpredictable time," he told her. "And, yes, it was fascinating too." He rested his cheek on top of her head. "At any rate, all this talk about Liam is pure speculation, as we have virtually nothing else to compare him to."

"We'll just have to accept whatever the future brings us, and it's okay," she murmured. "I'll adjust. The main thing is that he's healthy and happy." Tilting back her head, she gave him a wry smile. "One thing's for sure—it's never dull around here, is it?"

His sexy mouth widened. "No, it never is."

"Anyway, I'm sorry I interrupted your meeting."

He cupped the back of her head in one big hand. "You should always interrupt me. If I'm in the middle of something urgent that can't be put on hold, I'll let you know."

Her gaze slid over to one corner of his office. Crates and stacks of books dominated that area of the room. The large round conference table was piled high with even more books, and there were more crates waiting his attention in the library.

Since July, Dragos had spent a virtual fortune on a variety of books on history and politics, both human and Elder Races, and the subject of each cluster of books focused on the gaps he had discovered in his memory.

Along with reading obsessively late into the night, he spent long hours talking to each of the sentinels, while major corporate decisions had been put on hold. His businesses, along with the Wyr demesne itself, were treading water but not making any forward strides.

Thankfully, they had the most active time of the political season behind them for the year. Dragos's assistants, especially Kris, were dedicated to the point of obsession, and with the sentinels' help, Dragos could afford to take time to concentrate on his own healing.

She asked, "How is it going?"

"Nothing new." He growled, "I'm learning a lot."

The frustration was evident in his voice. During the first few weeks of his recovery, he'd had several strong episodes of spontaneous memory retrieval. Now he recalled almost everything from the last few years, but since then, he had discovered that he'd lost entire centuries, and it had been at least ten days since he'd had his last breakthrough.

And, as he was quick to point out, so much of what had really happened in history had never made it into any book. Most of Dragos's life, in fact, including any number of private wars, feuds, pacts, and betrayals.

Closing her eyes, she rubbed his wide, muscled back. "I'm so sorry."

And she was. She was terribly sorry about his frustration, and she understood how the whole experience contributed to him looking at the world through even more distrustful eyes. He believed that they were more vulnerable now, and what he didn't know could possibly hurt them one day.

But in a way, she couldn't relate. She didn't care about what had happened that far in the past. All that really mattered to her was that he was hers again, that he remembered her, that he had regained his physical health and he loved and needed her as much as he ever had.

The Wyr demesne was strong. They had all kinds of help and protection, and they could rebuild anything else.

She asked, "Is there anything I can do to help?"

He buried his nose in her hair, took a deep breath and sighed. "You help just by being here."

"Well, that bit is easy," she told him with a smile. "Because I wouldn't be anywhere else." After a pause, she added more gently, "I do get concerned sometimes at how hard you're working. It's only been a month since you got hurt, so you might very well have more memories return. But I hope you can come to terms with the fact that you might not, either."

"I'll cross that bridge when I come to it," he said. The tone of his voice had turned dark and edged. "But I'm not there yet, and in the meantime, I won't let go of a single moment of my life without a fight."

That ferocity of his was one of the very things that had drawn her to him in the first place. He wouldn't let go of anything of his without a fight. And he was the meanest, nastiest fighter she knew.

Drawing comfort from that now, she lifted her head, and he responded readily, cupping her chin and covering her mouth with his, until everything else fell away in the brightness of the fire they created together.

Chapter Three

SCHOOL WAS EVERY bit as interesting as Liam thought it would be.

Well, actually the *schooling* bit wasn't very interesting, but Mom and Dad had already warned him that he would know a lot more than other first graders. Be patient, they had said. Your school experience is going to be different from everyone else's.

Everything else was awesome.

His teacher's name was Mrs. Teaberry, and she was pretty old. He couldn't tell what exactly Mrs. Teaberry was—he wasn't very good yet at identifying other peoples' natures—but she might be part Fae. Her hair was gray, and she had interesting lines on her face that moved around as her expression changed.

There were twenty kids in his class, and he watched them with fascination. Some were boisterous and excited, and others seemed timid and shy. One of them cried quietly for a few minutes, hiding it behind one hand. He felt bad for her, but as he sat across the classroom from her, there was nothing he could do to help.

There was no sign of the Dark Fae girl, so she must be in another class. He was sorry about that, as he liked how her eyes sparkled.

The teacher talked a lot, and he got bored and stopped paying attention. His gaze wandered over to a collection of books she had on a bookcase in one corner, behind her desk. Those weren't kids' books. Those were adult books, with titles that contained words like *learning methodology*, and *first-grade literacy*.

He had never read anything like those books before, and they piqued his interest.

When morning recess came, he slipped out of line, doubled back into the classroom and went to explore the teacher's books. He had flipped through almost all of them when Mrs. Teaberry walked back into the empty classroom.

The wrinkles on her face shifted into an expression of surprise. "Liam," she said. "What on earth are you doing? You're supposed to be outside with everybody else."

He closed the last book and slid it back on the shelf. "I wanted to read your books first."

She laughed. "You mean you're done looking at them. They're a bit too old for you."

Turning, he cocked his head at her. "No, I read them. I'm done now."

Her eyes narrowed, and her smile faded into something much more stern. "I don't appreciate someone who tells tall tales. You didn't read all of those books in just a few minutes. You should have said that you were just looking at them."

Confused, he blinked. He wasn't telling any tall tales.

Was she . . . calling him a liar? He wasn't sure. Nobody had ever called him a liar before.

"No," he said again, patiently. "I read them."

He waited for her to ask him questions about the books, which was what Mom and Dad would have done.

Instead, her expression turned cold, and her voice sharpened. "Go outside, young man. We'll talk about this later."

Talk about what later?

More confused than ever, and growing a little angry, he did as he was told and went outside.

There were so many kids, many more than just from his classroom. All the classes were out, including the older ones. He stood still, absorbing the scene.

The morning had turned sunny and hot, and puffy white clouds floated around in the sky. Tilting his face up to the sunlight, he wanted very badly to join the clouds in flight, but that wasn't what he was supposed to be doing.

Somewhere, just off the school grounds, Hugh and other guards kept watch, but they were well hidden from sight. He thought about calling Hugh to say hi, but his phone was supposed to be for emergencies only, and he didn't think feeling lonely was an emergency.

In the playground, some kids were running and shouting, and others climbed on the jungle gyms. Still others were swinging on the swing set, and he noticed a few squatting and digging at the base of one of the trees.

Late as he was in joining recess, he wasn't exactly sure how to participate. Was he supposed to run around and shout, or climb on the jungle gyms? He didn't feel like doing any of that, so he went in search of the Dark Fae girl instead.

It took him a while, because she wasn't easy to find, which made him curious and even more interested. His hunting instincts engaged, he started to look in less obvious, more out-of-the-way places.

There were a surprising number of places that were less obvious and out-of-the-way, such as behind trees, or down a bare concrete stairwell. Rounding the corner of the building, he found the Dark Fae girl in the middle of a tense scene.

He took everything in at once. There were four boys, along with the girl. One boy knelt on the ground, sniffling.

The Dark Fae girl shoved one of the three boys. "Leave him alone!"

The boy shoved her back, hard, making her stumble, while the last two boys closed around her in a circle. "I've told you before to stay out of this," the first boy hissed. "Stop sticking your nose in where it doesn't belong."

Liam felt his eyebrows go up. He didn't have a clue what all that was about, but the predator in him instinctively recognized how the three boys were acting. They were trying to act like the Dark Fae girl was prey, but clearly she wasn't having any of it.

The fourth boy though, the one on the ground, was acting quite a bit like prey. He was smaller than the others, more delicately built, and fear poured off him in waves.

Liam looked at him for a long moment. While he might act like prey, he wasn't a wild animal or a cow. He was a person. Liam thought he might be human, while the other three boys were some kind of Wyr.

The Dark Fae girl balled her hands into fists. Violence hovered in the air, an invisible and yet very real presence.

Hands in the pockets of his khaki shorts, Liam touched the tip of his phone with one finger but left it alone.

He said, "Hi, guys. What's up?"

The boy that the Dark Fae girl had shoved spun around, angrily. He said, "None of your business. Butt out."

Liam gave the human boy another thoughtful glance. His cheek was reddened. It looked like somebody had hit him.

Liam's attention went back to the boy who told him to butt out. Was he a ringleader? Liam always wondered what it might be like to meet a ringleader.

He said, "I don't think so. I think you need to stop what you're doing."

Ringleader Boy stared. "Are you stupid?"

"No." He darted a glance at the Dark Fae girl. "I don't believe I am."

The expression on her face, he had to admit, was a bit skeptical.

Ringleader Boy stepped forward, his posture aggressive and the expression in his eyes flat. The other two boys flanked him on either side. Liam recognized what they were doing. Dad had talked about it before. He called it pack behavior.

Ringleader Boy said, "Yeah, well, I think you're pretty stupid."

Interesting things were going on in Liam's body. He felt flushed and twitchy, at once angry and very alert.

He felt like violence might be a good thing.

Pulling his hands out of his pockets, Liam walked up to Ringleader Boy. He didn't stop until his chest bumped the other boy's chest hard enough to knock him back. Astonishment took over Ringleader Boy's face. His fist flashed up, shooting toward Liam's face.

Liam realized he was a lot faster than the other boy, and he had plenty of time to do something. As he watched Ringleader Boy's fist coming toward him, he tried to decide what he was supposed to do.

In the meantime, everything inside him seemed to be racing harder, faster. He felt his heart pounding as if he had been running, and he liked it. It felt good.

He brought up one arm and blocked the punch on his way to taking Ringleader Boy by the throat. The other boy's expression turned shocked, and he coughed.

Around them, the Dark Fae girl and the two other boys shifted. One of them swore. The human boy crawled several feet, stood and ran away.

None of that mattered. Liam looked Ringleader Boy in the eye. You, he thought. You're prey.

You're my prey.

Ringleader Boy's eyes widened, and fear crept in to

join the ugliness.

Liam's cell phone rang, splintering the moment.

For a moment, he didn't move. It felt too good to have a grip on Ringleader Boy's throat. Then his phone rang again, and only three people in the entire world had his number—Hugh, Mom or Dad—so he let go of Ringleader Boy to reach inside his pocket.

As he did, the other boy's face twisted. Rubbing his throat, he snapped, "You're not supposed to have a cell phone in school."

As Liam watched, Ringleader Boy skipped backward to join his two friends, and they all raced away, disappearing around the corner of the school building.

Pulling out his phone, he answered it. "Hello?"

Hugh asked in a gentle, easygoing tone of voice, "Hi, Liam. What are you doing, buddy?"

Just the fact that he asked that question made Liam think Hugh knew what he was doing. Liam lifted his head and looked around. He couldn't see Hugh, but that didn't mean that Hugh couldn't see him.

Rubbing the back of his head, he said, "It's kind of hard to explain."

"Everything all right?"

"Sure, I guess." Turning on his heel, he looked around. Everyone was gone except for the Dark Fae girl, who watched him with large, wary eyes. He told Hugh, "I got really mad at somebody, and I almost lost my temper."

"But you didn't."

"No." But he could have. He had been awfully close.

Did that make him bad? Honesty forced him to admit, "Not this time anyway."

Hugh didn't sound shocked or worried. In fact, he sounded as mild as ever. "Good job, sport. You okay?"

"Yeah. I think so."

"Call if you need to."

"I will."

He hung up and said to the Dark Fae girl, "Hi, my name's Liam."

He kind of wanted to add the Double Oh Peanut and Rock Star stuff, but he didn't think she would find it as funny as he had the first time.

She didn't say hi back. She said, "I'm Marika." She pointed to the phone. "First, that's gonna get you into trouble. You're in Mrs. Teaberry's class, right?"

"Yeah."

"She can be really mean if you get on her bad side. She's made kids cry before."

He pocketed it. "I'm supposed to carry my phone at all times, so it's gonna have to be okay."

Shaking her head, Marika said, "Second, those boys? They're not going to forgive or forget what you just did. You're pretty big for a first grader, and you're really, *really* fast. In fact you might be faster than any kid I've ever seen, plus you look strong. But they're third graders, and now you're on their shit list, and that's not a good place to be." She scowled and muttered *damn it* under her breath. "Sorry. I know I'm not supposed to swear at school."

Starting to feel entertained, Liam put his hands in his

pockets again and rocked on the balls of his feet.

"It's okay," he told her, thinking of the sentinels, and of Hugh and Eva. And of Mom too, on occasion, but especially Dad. "I live with a bunch of people who swear a lot."

Marika looked at him sidelong again, as if she wasn't sure he had all his marbles. "Look, I'm trying to tell you something. You made some bad kids really mad at you just now."

Actually, he wasn't sure how to respond to that. He was running into a lot of new situations today. Rubbing the back of his head again, he thought about it. *Cool* didn't seem like quite the right thing to say, so his mind wandered off on a different tangent. "Who were they, and why were they bullying that other boy?"

She paused as if he had surprised her. Then she said, "Andrew is the guy who tried to punch you. He's the leader."

Oh yes. Ringleader Boy. He nodded.

"Joel and Brad are tools. They just do everything Andrew says, but that doesn't mean they do nothing. Perrin is the kid they were picking on. We're all in the same class. Perrin did something really stupid last year—when he saw them breaking into the teacher's lounge, he told on them. They got in major trouble and they weren't allowed to go to the end of the year picnic, and now they won't leave him alone."

"What did they do?"

Her face tightened. "I told you, they're really bad. They stole money and ruined his lunch several times.

They tore up his homework, and beat him up a couple times. Once his mom had to take him to the hospital for stitches. I told Perrin he had started something he had to finish, and he needed to tell his mom and dad who had hurt him, but he got too scared and stopped talking. Summer break is a long time. I thought they would have moved on to something else by now." Then her wide, gray gaze locked onto him, and her expression changed. "Since you've butted in, they probably have."

"You mean they'll start picking on me," he said.

She looked exasperated. "That's what I'm trying to tell you."

"Okay, thanks for the warning," he told her. He still liked her, but he had to admit, she seemed pretty grumpy. "What about you? You stuck up for Perrin too."

She looked angry and a bit lost. "I have to. He's my neighbor, and we've sort of grown up together. We had to play together when we were little. And he doesn't have a clue about how *anything* works."

So she recognized Perrin as prey too. Liam blew out a breath. "So, they don't leave you alone either?"

"Like I said, that's probably changed, thanks to you crashing their party. It's hard to believe you found so much trouble in your first recess."

It didn't seem like the best time to tell her he'd been looking for her.

Her head turned in the direction of the larger play area. "Look, I gotta go. Try not to be too stupid, will you?"

That sounded like some great advice. As she ran off,

he called after her, "Thanks, I'll try."

The recess bell rang, and everybody ran to get in their line for class. For a few minutes, the playground swirled with confusion as kids pushed past each other, searching for the right place to get in line.

Something hit Liam between the shoulder blades, hard enough to send him down on one knee. Coughing in surprise at the sharp pain, he went forward, splaying his hands on the asphalt in front of him.

Then a blaze of energy shot through him. Breathing hard, he leaped to his feet and whirled, looking around. He couldn't see Andrew or either of the tools, Joel and Brad. Other children surrounded him. The babble of their voices seemed too loud and shrill. Nobody was paying attention to him, or looked like they thought anything was odd, but he knew what happened.

That hadn't been an ordinary shove. Someone had hit him, hard.

Nobody had ever hit him before.

He rotated his shoulders to ease the ache, while blood pounded through his body. It was another good lesson.

As strong and fast as he was, someone could still strike him in the back and hurt him bad, and if he didn't keep his guard up, he might never see it coming.

The rest of the morning dragged on. Mrs. Teaberry didn't smile at him or call on him, no matter how many times he raised his hand when she asked questions. She always picked somebody else to answer, until finally Liam stopped raising his hand altogether.

Perplexed, he studied her. She almost acted as if she were mad at him, or as if she didn't like him. He didn't know quite what to make of that. Usually, people liked him, but school had turned out to be much trickier than he had expected.

He was happy when lunchtime came. He would have gone to look for Marika, if he could have, but they were supposed to stay in line as they got their trays and went to sit at the long tables. Hungrily he ate all of his food, even though some of it was unappetizing.

After the meal, they went outside for another recess. The day had turned hot, and some of the other kids gathered in the shade of the large trees, but he liked the warm sunshine and basked in it.

The area between his shoulder blades, where somebody had hit him, still ached, and he rotated his shoulders. Sally, the girl he had sat by at lunch, asked, "Wanna play hopscotch?"

Just then, he caught sight of Andrew, Brad and Joel. They hung on the metal railing that bordered the concrete stairwell. As they talked, all three looked at him.

Andrew met his gaze. The other boy's eyes were narrowed and cold, and the sore spot between Liam's shoulders throbbed.

He said to Sally, "Thanks, but not right now. Maybe tomorrow."

"Okay." She walked away.

He watched as Sally joined a couple of other girls, and they started a new game of hopscotch. Then he looked back at Andrew and the tools.

While he had been looking away, one of the tools, Brad, had disappeared. Andrew and Joel leaned their elbows on the railing, still watching him.

Liam's heart kicked. On reflex, he spun in a circle, but Brad was nowhere in sight. Andrew smiled at him, and it wasn't a nice expression.

It was obvious they were planning something, but what? Liam didn't know. He was starting to feel twitchy again, and after giving that first big kick of surprise, his heart kept pounding, only this time it didn't feel good. This time, he didn't have any idea what he should do or where he should go.

Was this how Perrin had felt, when the three other boys had bullied him?

As Liam stared at Andrew, a slow, wild anger started to burn through his uncertainty.

I'm not prey. *I will never be prey.*

But he could still be hurt.

They could still hurt him. They could still hurt other kids.

When Andrew crooked a finger at him in unmistakable invitation, he started forward. He glanced around at the buildings and the open land on the other side of the school fence. He still couldn't see Hugh or any of the other guards.

Moving toward the other boy, he slipped one hand into his pocket.

And turned off his phone.

Chapter Four

THE SUN FELT hot on his head and shoulders as he crossed the asphalt expanse toward the other two boys, and he burned with energy.

He also had plenty of time to think things over, just as he had when Andrew had tried to punch him at morning recess.

What am I going to do? What should I do?

Maybe those were two separate things.

Other questions occurred to him. What would Dad do? Or Uncle Graydon, or Hugh? Or Mom?

Trying to figure that out was much trickier than trying to hold on to a cloaking spell. They were all very different people, which meant they might make very different choices from each other.

Maybe that meant there was more than one right way to deal with something, and maybe . . . more than one wrong way to deal with something too.

To be sure he dealt with this in the right way, he might have to grow up some more. His dragon side liked that idea and tried to *push* to get bigger, but he managed to stay in control of that for now. Eventually his dragon side would win and he would go through another growth spurt, but he could postpone it for a while.

The only thing he knew for sure was that dealing with cows was easy compared to dealing with Andrew and the tools. As Hugh had said about the cows (or hunting any other kind of prey), take only what you need, kill them quick and don't let them suffer.

When he reached the stairwell the other boys straightened from the railing and started over to him, both walking with a bit of a swagger and darting glances at each other.

Were they egging each other on? Where had Brad gone?

Giving the area outside the playground one last glance, Liam jogged lightly down the bare, concrete steps in the stairwell. There was nothing at the bottom of the stairs except for a few dried leaves, and a metal, locked door that led into the school building.

Nobody would be able to see what happened down here, unless Hugh or one of the other guards flew directly overhead, which they might choose to do, but he hoped not. He wanted to figure this out on his own.

Turning, he put the concrete wall at his back and looked up at the other two boys who stood at the top of the stairs. Then the predator in him went quiet and waited.

Come on, he thought. I was fast earlier, and that surprised you, but I'm just a first grader and you guys are third graders. There's only one of me, while there's two of you.

Andrew and Joel must have arrived at the same conclusion, because after exchanging a grin, they bounded down the stairs after him.

Okay, then. He got ready.

Andrew said, "How's your back? I heard you fell down earlier and got a boo-boo."

Joel snickered.

"Maybe you'll fall down again someday soon," said Andrew. The expression in his eyes had turned hectic, and he looked excited. "Maybe you'll get more than just a boo-boo. Maybe you'll lose some real blood."

Anger flared, bright and hot like the summer sun. Liam leaped at the other two boys, and before they could do anything, he shoved them against the wall, one hand around each of their throats. Shock bolted over their faces, as they slapped and kicked him.

He was too mad to really feel the blows. Leaning his weight on his arms, he held them pinned in place, and he felt the flutter of their pulses in his hands.

"I don't know why you need to bully other kids," he said. He thought of the teacher's books he had read that morning and some of the potential causes for disruptive behavior. "Maybe you're going through a rough time, or maybe you're just plain nasty. I don't like any of you, so I don't really care."

Andrew hit at Liam again. "You're making a serious mistake," he growled. "There are three of us and only one of you, and I will *hurt you bad* for this."

Liam's anger burst into outright rage. Leaning harder on his hands, he stuck his face into Andrew's and hissed.

Heat boiled out of his mouth, along with a lick of flame. It startled him so badly he stopped doing it.

Did I just breathe fire in my human form?

The other two boys quit struggling and stared. Andrew breathed, "What kind of Wyr *are* you?"

"Uh," said Joel. Tears ran down his cheeks. "Uh, uh, uh. I never meant any of it. Swear to God. *He* made me do it." He jerked his head toward Andrew.

Liam started to feel bad that he made someone else cry, but he forced himself to toughen up. None of them had gone easy on Perrin, or, he suspected, Marika either.

"Swear you'll stop," Liam told him. "Leave Perrin and Marika alone. Don't pick on anybody else, ever again."

"I swear," said Joel.

Letting him go, Liam wiped his hand on his shorts. As Joel raced up the stairs, Liam turned his attention to Andrew, whom he still held pinned.

He told the other boy, "You can try hitting me in the back again or hurting me some other way, but I know to watch out for you now, and anything you try is only going to make me mad. If you don't stop hurting people, I'll come find you. I'll hunt you down. That's what I'm made for, hunting things. And when I find you, I'll pound your face into the sidewalk."

Joel had gone red, but Andrew's face turned chalk white. His eyes darting around the stairwell, he whispered uncertainly, "You wouldn't dare."

"I can start now, if you want," said Liam.

Moving too fast for the other boy to stop him, he flipped Andrew around. Bracing one hand at the back of the other boy's head, he pushed Andrew's face hard against the concrete wall.

Andrew cried out, "Okay, okay—I believe you! I swear, I'll stop! *I'll stop!*"

Breathing hard, Liam listened closely to what Andrew said. Like his ability to identify a person's nature, his truthsense wasn't very well developed yet, but he could still hear the ring of truth in the other boy's voice.

The thing was, Liam still didn't believe him. He thought Joel would probably keep his word, but Andrew seemed different from Brad and Joel. There was something wrong with Andrew, something really bad that ran deep. He might stop for a while until he stopped believing that he would get caught, but sooner or later Liam thought he would hurt somebody again, because he liked hurting people too much.

But Liam wasn't old enough to fix anything like that. The only thing he could do was scare Andrew badly enough to make sure that future stayed far away.

Leaning forward to put his lips near Andrew's ear, he tried another hiss. Heat boiled out between his lips again and singed the ends of the other boy's hair. Crying out, Andrew cringed against the wall.

That would have to do. Satisfied, he let him go, and Andrew bolted for the stairs.

Turning to follow the other boy, Liam climbed the stairs, and as he looked up he discovered Marika hanging over the railing and staring down at him. She wore a solemn expression, and her gray eyes were huge.

He reached the top stair and sat down, stretching his legs out and looking at them. He had collected a couple of bruises on his shins where the other boys had kicked him. They would fade quickly enough, hopefully before the end of the day.

The angry energy was leaving him. He felt his dragon side straining to get bigger again, and this time he had to struggle to stay in control. After not having much of an appetite for a couple of meals, he felt hollow and empty. He wanted some meat, but he wouldn't get a snack until after school, so he resigned himself to feeling hungry for a few hours.

Marika came to sit beside him. She tucked sleek black hair behind one pointed ear, as she said, "That was hella awesome. Excuse my French."

His cheeks warmed. "They needed to be stopped."

"Yeah, I know, or one of these days, they were going to hurt somebody really bad." She studied him for a moment. "You did a good thing. And dude, you breathed fire!"

"I guess I did, didn't I?" He gave Marika a sidelong smile. She smiled back. On impulse, he said, "Hey, would you like to be my girlfriend for a couple of days?"

A startled wash of color stained her pale cheeks. She stared at him. "Only for a couple of days?"

He had forgotten—she didn't know who he really was, or anything about him. "Or maybe a week. It's kind of hard to explain," he told her. "I'm not going to be a kid for very long, so I can't make any long-term commitments."

She laughed. "You really are strange, you know that? What kind of Wyr breathes fire?"

There was a pebble stuck in the sole of his shoe, and he reached down to pick at it. "My kind, I guess."

"Seriously, are you keeping it a secret?"

As he opened his mouth to tell her he didn't know if it was a secret or not, a tall, strange girl ran up to them. She was one of the older kids. She asked, "Are you Liam Giovanni?"

He nodded.

"Mrs. Teaberry said to tell you to come into the classroom now."

Disappointed, he glanced at Marika, who might or might not be his girlfriend. "But recess isn't over yet."

The strange girl lifted one shoulder. "Not my problem. Teacher wants to talk to you."

Sighing, he stood, and Marika did too. She grinned at him. "Yes."

It took him a moment to realize what she meant. Then happiness made him grin back. "Really?"

"Yes, weirdo. Really. See you later." She punched him lightly on the shoulder and took off.

He said to the strange girl, "I'm dating an older woman now."

Not bothering with a verbal reply, the strange girl curled a nostril at him before she took off too.

Cheerfully, Liam made his way back to the classroom. It was funny how everything had been so strange at the beginning of the day, but he knew where he was going now, and the hallways and the classrooms seemed familiar.

When he walked into his classroom, it was empty

except for Mrs. Teaberry, who was in one corner stacking plastic tubs filled with supplies on top of each other.

He asked, "You wanted to talk to me?"

Straightening, she turned to face him, and the lines on her face didn't look friendly at all. "Yes, I did," she said. "We have two issues we need to settle. First, you need to know that liars won't do very well in my class. They won't do very well at all."

His cheerfulness faded into confusion. More than a little disturbed, he cocked his head. "Are you talking about me?"

Looking exasperated, she said, "Of course I am. Surely you haven't forgotten that you claimed to have read my entire bookshelf in a matter of minutes."

Clenching his hands, he said through his teeth, "But I did."

She pointed at him. "You need to tell the truth right now and admit you were lying."

His mouth dropped open, and he stared at her. "You want me to do what?"

"You have to change your behavior, or I promise you, you're going to have a very tough first year, which leads me to the second issue we need to address. I heard you have a cell phone, and you were taking phone calls during morning recess. That's against school policy, and you'll have to give it up." She walked toward him, holding out her hand.

His mind flashed back to earlier, when Andrew and Joel had been watching him with such satisfied smiles, while Brad had disappeared from sight. Marika had said his phone would get him into trouble, and it looked like the other boys had made sure of it.

As Mrs. Teaberry approached, he backed away. "I can't. I'm supposed to keep my phone with me at all times."

"Unacceptable. Give it to me right now." She wiggled her fingers at him demandingly.

Shaking his head, he said again, "I can't."

Her expression turned incredulous and angry. "You're in big trouble, young man. This is my classroom, and in here, other rules don't apply. You do as I tell you. Hand it over."

Nobody had ever said such a thing to him before. And anyway, he didn't believe it. Dad's rules applied everywhere.

His body turned very hot, then cold. This felt completely unlike what had happened with the other boys. With them, he had acted on instinct, a certain amount of predatory cunning and on snippets he had heard about how the sentinels handled problems, but Mrs. Teaberry was an adult and his teacher.

He was supposed to mind her, but he also couldn't go against the safety rules. Starting to tremble, he shook his head. "No."

Mrs. Teaberry's eyes flashed. Lunging forward, she grabbed him by the shoulder.

Shocked, Liam tried to twist away, but her grip on him was too strong. "If you won't give it to me," Mrs. Teaberry said, "I'll just have to take it."

She rammed one hand into his pocket, searching for the phone. He struggled against her hold. "Stop—you can't do that. I'm supposed to keep it with me."

Her fingers dug into his shoulder like claws, and she shook him. "Everybody always thinks the rules don't apply to them," she snapped. "But they do. They apply to you too, mister."

He couldn't let her take the phone, and she was hurting him. She was scaring him too. He couldn't call Hugh. He had turned his phone off. He couldn't call Mom or Dad, either.

Feeling invaded and trapped, he felt his fingers change and his teeth lengthen into fangs. He rounded on Mrs. Teaberry with a snarl.

She recoiled from him. Almost immediately, she straightened until she stood very erect. Her tight mouth bit out words. *"Don't you dare bite me, you little animal."*

Trembling more violently than ever, he swiped at his face as he looked at her hands. She clenched his phone in one fist.

Breathing hard, he angled out his jaw and said, "Give it back."

Astonishment took over her expression. She shook the phone at him. "I said you can't have it in school."

Growling, he walked toward her. She retreated until her back came up against a wall. Dimly, he was aware that his face was still not right. He had too many teeth, and they felt sharp against his tongue. When he held out one hand, palm up, he saw that it was tipped with long, sharp talons.

Cautiously, her eyes wide, Mrs. Teaberry set the phone in his palm.

As he turned it on, he thought about calling Hugh, because he wanted to see a friendly face as soon as possible. Then he thought about calling Mom, because he needed her to love on him and tell him everything was going to be okay.

But really, he had screwed up in so many ways that day, the only thing to do was to take it straight to the top.

He pressed rapid-dial number two.

Dad answered before the first ring had ended. "What's going on, Liam?"

Taking a deep breath, he said, "Can you come pick me up? I think I'm about to get expelled."

Chapter Five

DRAGOS CHANGED INTO his dragon form, since flying directly to the school was much faster than driving on the winding country roads. Pia rode on his back, muttering worriedly. She asked, *Did he tell you what happened?*

No, Dragos said, which was the strict truth.

He didn't mention what Hugh had already told him about Liam's two confrontations at recess. While Dragos planned on telling Pia everything, he still hadn't figured out what to say about those incidents.

He was proud as hell of how his son had handled the bullies, and he was both surprised and intrigued at Liam's newly emerged talent for breathing fire in his human form, but Dragos wasn't sure that Pia would feel the same way. Sometimes family dynamics were an interesting puzzle.

He also planned on having Andrew and his family investigated. As Hugh pointed out, the boy might need counseling or even special schooling.

Dragos kept his cloaking spell tight around them until after he had landed and shapeshifted back into his human form. Taking Pia's hand, they strode quickly into the school building and to the administrative offices.

The school secretary escorted them into the principal's office. Inside, the principal, Doreen Chambers, waited with an older woman, and with Liam.

Dragos took in everything about the older woman at a glance. She was of mixed race, part human and part Dark Fae, and she wore a tight-lipped, self-righteous expression. He turned his attention to his son, who sat with such quiet dignity that it took Dragos a moment to realize Liam was trembling. He clutched his phone tightly in both hands and didn't look at either the principal or the older woman.

A silent snarl built at the back of Dragos's throat. As Pia rushed to Liam, Dragos rounded on the other two women. He said in a quiet, rigidly controlled voice, "Explain this."

As the older woman had caught sight of him and Pia, her expression had changed. Clearly she recognized them. Instead of looking self-righteous, she started to look worried.

She should.

Doreen Chambers walked around her desk, hand outstretched to Dragos. She said, "Lord and Lady Cuelebre, this is Liam's teacher, Elora Teaberry. I owe all of you a profound apology. You see, we have a policy that children aren't allowed to have cell phones at school. . . . And with everything involved with the start of the school year, I simply forgot to tell Elora that we would make an exception in Liam's case."

Dragos ignored the principal's outstretched hand. Instead, he focused on Liam's teacher. Not only had her expression changed, but she was starting to smell nervous too.

On its own, that wouldn't be enough to pique his interest, because people smelled nervous around him all the time. However, when he combined her nervousness with Liam's upset, he didn't like the picture that was starting to emerge.

Elora Teaberry's chin came up. "Mr. and Mrs. Cuelebre," she said stiffly. "Had I been told that your son would be in my class, things might have gone very differently. As it was, I insisted he give me his cell phone, and he growled and snapped at me. I'm sure I don't have to tell you that this is not acceptable or safe behavior—"

Tuning her out, Dragos turned to Pia and Liam. Whispering soft words of comfort, Pia squatted by Liam's chair. His head lowered, Liam turned in his chair to lean toward her. Pia slipped an arm around him, cupped his shoulder and squeezed.

With an indrawn hiss and a grimace, Liam pulled away from her hug, and everything in the room changed drastically.

Frowning, Pia asked him sharply, "What's the matter, sweetheart—are you hurt anywhere?"

Liam muttered, "Not really. It's okay."

Pia's eyes flashed to Dragos. Shifting so that she crouched in front of Liam and blocked him from the rest of the room, she went silent. Liam looked at her, nodded then shook his head. They had gone telepathic. She eased the neckline of his shirt to one side to reveal bruises in the shape of fingermarks on one slim shoulder.

"Oh my God," said the principal, blanching.

Dragos's silent snarl turned audible. Pia whirled to face Elora Teaberry, her expression blazing with incredulous rage. "You put your hands on him. *You shook him?*"

The teacher's nervousness turned to outright fear, and her gaze darted around the room. "Everything I did was in self-defense. Your son snarled at me—he acted like he would bite me. He had partially shapeshifted, and he had claws and teeth—"

Liam said in a clear, strong voice, "You're a liar. You're lying."

Sliding out of his chair, he stood beside Pia's crouching figure and put his arm around her. To Dragos's eyes, it looked like a protective stance. Liam was guarding his mother.

Reining in his own rage so that he could at least appear calm, Dragos asked Liam, "What really happened?"

Liam said, "Well, first she said, you couldn't have read all those books, you're a liar. And I said, I did too read them, but she never asked me about learning methodology or first-grade literacy, or anything about what was really in the books. Then she said, it's against the rules to have a cell phone, so you give it to me right now, young man, and I said no, I can't do that, it's against the rules. So she grabbed me, and I tried to fight her off, and she shook me, and that's when I got toothy, and she said, *Don't you dare bite me, you little animal.*" He was breathing hard, and his eyes flashed with dark violet fire. "And she got my phone out of my pocket, so I said, give it back. And she gave it back. That's when I called you."

When he finished, a stark silence fell as everyone stared at Elora Teaberry, who stood with her back pressed against the wall. "That's not what happened," she said faintly. "He growled first. He snapped at me. He thought the rules didn't apply to him!"

Dragos could hear the lie in her voice. It was so apparent he felt sure the other two women could hear it too.

The principal's expression was appalled, while Pia looked more murderous than Dragos had ever seen her, and he knew fully well that he had the teacher's death stamped in the lines of his own face.

"This is so far beyond anything appropriate or acceptable, I have no words," breathed the principal.

"Well, you'd better come up with a few," Pia snarled as she surged to her feet. "And 'I'm so desperately sorry' and 'We're going to press charges' better be some of the first words out of your mouth."

It was so charming how Pia's thinking went straight to the justice system, while he thought of things like vivisection and dismemberment.

Dragos's gaze dropped to Liam. Now that he had told his story, the boy looked completely calm, even analytical, as he regarded Elora Teaberry. He had stopped shaking, and all signs of his previous upset had vanished.

What was going on in that brilliant, unpredictable,

dangerous young mind of his?

Dragos decided to find out. He asked telepathically, *What do you think should happen to Mrs. Teaberry?*

Liam's gaze lifted to his. *Other kids warned me she would be mean. I want to know if she's hurt anybody else.*

Dragos lifted his eyebrows. *That's an excellent point*, he said. *I think we should find out, and if she has, we need to contact those children's parents.*

Liam nodded. He had slipped his arm around Pia's waist, and he leaned against her again. His expression was serious. *We need to make sure those kids are okay.*

Liam had been hurt, and he'd been upset and frightened enough that he had partially shapeshifted, but his first thought afterward had been for other children.

A powerful wave of pride conquered Dragos's rage. Already, his son was a far better man than he would ever be.

Walking over to Pia and Liam, he asked gently, *Are you all right?*

The boy gave him a faint smile, and Dragos got a glimpse of the older soul inhabiting that young body. *Yeah. I didn't let her keep my phone.*

He stroked Liam's bright, silken hair. *Good boy.*

"Oh, I almost forgot," Liam said aloud. He looked up at his mom and gave her a crooked grin. "I've got a girlfriend."

Dragos wished he could have taken a photo of that moment, because the look on Pia's face was priceless.

✧   ✧   ✧

MAYBE THINGS DIDN'T completely and totally suck after all.

A couple of the guards who had been watching over the school with Hugh came to take Mrs. Teaberry away, but not before Dad stood in the corner with her for a long time in silence. Liam never found out what Dad said to her, but whatever it was, it turned her skin pasty white and made her hands shake.

Briefly, Liam thought he might feel bad about that, but then he didn't. Sorry, not sorry.

After the guards took Mrs. Teaberry out of the room, Mom, Dad, Mrs. Chambers and he talked. Mom asked, "How do you feel about school now?"

"I like it!" he told her. It had been a busy first day, and going undercover was every bit as interesting as he thought it would be.

"Do you want to come back tomorrow?" Mom watched him closely.

"Yeah. Does that mean I get a new teacher?"

"It absolutely does," Dad said.

The adults talked for a while, and Liam lost interest. He wandered over to the bookcases that Mrs. Chambers had in her office, and he read a couple of books until they were finished. Mrs. Chambers said, "There'll be a substitute teacher in his class until I can hire someone else. Again, I can't tell you how sorry I am that this happened. Elora worked here for years, and I never heard a whisper of anything like this before."

Liam sneaked a look at Mom, who didn't look molli-fied. Her face set, she said, "Sometimes you only hear whispers if you listen for them well enough."

At that, Mrs. Chambers looked both terribly apologetic and rather offended, which Liam thought was a pretty hard expression to pull off. But she must have thought Mom had a point, because she didn't say anything.

Soon afterward, they left. Liam would have rather gone back into class, but Mom and Dad decided he'd had enough for one day. Outside, Eva leaned against the bumper of an SUV. Dad held out his hand, and Eva tossed the keys at him.

Dad said, "Thanks. Find your own way home, okay?"

"You got it," Eva said.

"I'm going to ride in the back with Liam," Mom said.

Dad smiled at them. "Good idea."

While he wouldn't have thought to ask for it, Liam was glad she did. They rode for a while quietly, and when he sneaked his hand into Mom's, she closed her fingers around his tightly.

Suddenly, she burst out, "I want to punch her evil, lying face."

Liam caught a flash of hot gold as Dad looked at them, narrow-eyed, in the rearview mirror. Dad said, completely seriously, "I can make that happen."

It wasn't really funny, and yet somehow it was. He burst out laughing, and after a few moments Mom and Dad laughed too. Mom raised his hand and kissed it. He wiggled sideways in his seat belt so he could lay his head on her shoulder, and in that moment, he felt completely happy.

She said, "I'm so sorry you ever had to go through that, but especially on your first day."

"I'm not," he told her.

She turned to him with a look of surprise. "Really?"

"Yeah. I mean, she made me mad and she sort of scared me for a few minutes, but it didn't last long, and she shouldn't be a teacher."

"Out of the mouth of babes," said Dad.

"What do you want for supper?" Mom asked him.

He replied, "Lots and lots of spaghetti. I'm starving."

She chuckled. "Dad and I might eat something else, but you can have spaghetti every night this week if you want."

So, in fact, everything turned out to be almost perfect.

Almost.

That night he ate so much spaghetti, Mom said he was in danger of turning into a big noodle, which made him laugh so hard, he fell out of his chair. The rest of the school week went well. The substitute teacher was wonderful, a smart and nice man named Mr. Huddleston. After a few days, Principal Chambers came into the classroom to announce that Mr. Huddleston would be their permanent teacher, and all the kids cheered.

Dad told him Mrs. Teaberry went to jail. It turned out she had been mean to other kids, and Dad said that lots of parents were pressing charges. Andrew, Brad and Joel stayed quiet at recess, and they left all the other kids alone.

Mom contacted Marika's and Perrin's parents, and one day, they came over for a playdate after school.

Liam had an awesome time. Perrin was an odd, nervous little nerd of a boy, but after he relaxed, he shouted and charged around with every bit as much energy as Marika did. They explored the woods behind the house and played pirates until the sun went down and the other kids had to go home.

So actually life could hardly have been better, except for one thing that weighed and weighed on his mind, until finally, on Friday evening, he couldn't take it any longer.

After supper, he and Mom made vegan rice crispy treats and together they ate the whole batch. Then, when Mom went upstairs to take a bath, he went in search of Dad and found him reading one of his history books in the library.

Liam wandered over to hang on the arm of his chair. Dad looked at him over the edge of his book. "Something on your mind?"

"Yeah. Maybe." Liam couldn't look into his dad's keen gaze, and he bent his head as he asked, "Can I talk to you in private?"

Dad glanced around the library, but instead of pointing out that the room was already empty except for them, after a moment he said, "Let's go for a walk."

Liam swallowed and nodded.

They went outside.

The sun had just set behind the nearby mountains, but it was still hot and plenty light enough. Overhead, the sky was streaked with rainbow colors. It would be a good evening to go flying, except Liam didn't feel like it.

Dad led him to the path that went to the lake, and soon they walked along the beach toward the half-completed office complex. It was the one place where Mom never came anymore.

Liam darted a thoughtful, uncertain glance up at Dad's face. While it was impossible to read Dad's expression, he felt pretty sure Dad hadn't picked the location by accident.

He said, experimentally, "I like the lake."

"I do too," said Dad. Stopping at a stack of concrete blocks, he sat on the edge of the pile and stretched his long legs out. He gave Liam a sidelong smile. "Don't worry, Mom will get over it. I think she'll come down here a lot once the building is completed and people move in. She doesn't let much hold her down, you know."

Liam nodded and turned to look out over the water, which reflected the rainbow colors in the sky. The lake blurred as his eyes filled, and his mouth wobbled as he asked, "Am I bad?"

In a very quiet voice, Dad asked, "Now, why would you think to ask such a thing?"

Squatting, he picked up a stick to poke at the ground, mostly to hide the fact that his tears had spilled over. "Last Sunday, when I was playing Spy Wyr, I heard you and Mom talking about how I needed school, so I could learn how to control myself."

Dad stayed silent a moment. He said, "We were on

the balcony. Where were you?"

"I climbed up to the beams u-underneath."

From the corner of his eye, he watched as Dad closed his eyes briefly and said to himself, "I didn't sense a damned thing."

He guessed that meant he'd gotten pretty good at his cloaking spell. Ducking his head, he said, "There were some bad boys at school. I made one of them cry, and I scared the other one pretty good. And I meant to. I . . . liked it. Oh—also, I can breathe fire. Watch."

Holding the stick to his lips, he concentrated on pulling on his Power as he hissed. Heat boiled out of his mouth, along with a lick of flame, and the stick caught fire.

"That's something, that is," said Dad in a soft voice. "Can you put it out?"

"Sure." He started to bury it in the dirt between his feet.

Dad took him gently by the wrist to stop him. "No, not that way. Try to put it out with your mind."

Liam looked at him uncertainly then focused on the stick. After a few moments, he said, "I don't think I can do that."

"That's okay, maybe you can't do it yet, but I'm sure you will be able to. We'll practice at it." Dad passed his hand over the stick and the tiny flame died down. "Okay, first things first. Come here."

As Liam stood up, Dad did something he didn't often do anymore. He picked Liam up like he was a little kid. Turning into the embrace, Liam wrapped his legs around Dad's waist and put his head on his shoulder.

Dad sat down again, holding him in a whole body hug. It felt good, like being surrounded by a hot, comforting fire. He rested his chin on Liam's shoulder. "Your mom and I already know about what happened with those other boys."

He mumbled, "You do?"

"Mm-hm. Hugh told us. After talking about it, we decided not to say anything unless you brought it up."

"Oh." After thinking about it, he whispered, "I'm not sorry."

Sorry, not sorry.

Dad rubbed his back. "You know what I think?"

He shook his head.

"I think you did an outstanding job."

Outstanding. He lifted his head. "Really?"

"Really. You spoke to them in their language. You backed them off, and you made them stop hurting other kids. And you controlled yourself, and you didn't hurt them in return."

He had to point out, "I scared them pretty bad."

"Yes, you did." Dad's face was calm. "If you were to talk to humans about this, they would probably say that things should be handled in a different way, and I respect that—but Liam, it's important to remember, we're not humans, and neither are those boys. They're stronger than humans, more dangerous. They're predators, and they crossed a line. You know what happens when Wyr go bad, don't you? They can hurt a lot of people before they're brought down."

"That's what the sentinels do," he said.

"That's right—that's part of what the sentinels do." Dad paused. "I also think it's important for you to remember, you have two sides to your nature. You have some of me in you, but you also have some of your mom too."

"That makes sense," he muttered.

"Your mom is much more peaceful than I am, so sometimes, you might find that those two sides are in conflict with each other. When that happens, you've got to give yourself time to think things over. You can always talk to either your mom or me. Between the three of us, I feel sure that we can sort things out. Okay?"

Blinking to clear his eyesight, he nodded. "Okay."

Dad looked over the water then back at him. "You know how old I am, right?"

"Yeah." It was actually hard to wrap his mind around the concept of just how old Dad was, but he had a general sort of idea.

Dad smiled at him. "In all of that time, you are the best thing I've ever done. You are the absolute best part of me, and I am so proud of you. Your mom is proud of you too, and she understands you better than you might think. You might be dangerous, but you could never, ever be bad. You just have to promise me one thing."

The weight lifted from his shoulders, until he felt light and free again. "What's that?"

"You've got to stop spying on adults, especially your mom and me. Sometimes we say things to each other that are private, and we say it in a way that the other person might understand, but nobody else would. It's called taking things in context. When you overhear stuff you're not supposed to hear, that's a good way to get your feelings hurt over nothing."

That made sense. He heaved a sigh. "Can I still play Spy Wyr with my friends?"

"Yes, you can."

"Okay. I promise I'll stop."

"Good boy. Are you ready to go back inside?"

"Yeah."

Dad hugged him tight then set him on his feet and stood.

As Liam looked up, his gaze caught on the thin white scar on Dad's forehead.

Dad was so big, so strong. He was stronger than anyone else Liam knew, but still . . . his dad could be hurt. As strong, old and fast as he was, someone could come at his back.

And Liam loved him so much it hurt. It was a good, deep ache.

When I finish getting big, he thought, I'm not ever going to let anything happen to you, or to Mom.

Not on my watch.

Dad held out his hand, and he took it. Together in the peaceful, deepening twilight, they walked back up to the house.

Thank you!

Dear Readers,

Thank you for reading my short story *Peanut Goes To School*. Dragos and Pia's son Liam is one of my favorite characters, and I'm delighted to share this story with you. I hope you had as much fun visiting with him as I did!

Would you like to stay in touch and hear about new releases? You can:

- Sign up for my monthly email at: www.theaharrison.com
- Follow me on Twitter at @TheaHarrison
- Like my Facebook page at http://facebook.com/TheaHarrison

Reviews help other readers find the books they like to read. I appreciate each and every review, whether positive or negative.

Peanut Goes To School is the final story in a three-story arc featuring Dragos, Pia and their son Liam (aka Peanut). The first story is *Dragos Takes a Holiday* (November, 2013 release), and the second is *Pia Saves The Day* (June, 2014 release).

Happy reading!
Thea

Also available:

Dragos Takes A Holiday
(A novella of the Elder Races)

The Bermuda Triangle. Pirates. The Peanut. What could possibly go wrong?

Dragos Cuelebre needs a vacation. So does Pia, his mate. When the First Family of the Wyr head to Bermuda for some much needed R&R, it's no ordinary undertaking – and no ordinary weekend in the sun. Between hunting for ancient treasure buried beneath the waves and keeping track of their son, Liam—a.k.a. Peanut, whose Wyr abilities are manifesting far ahead of schedule—it's a miracle that Pia and Dragos can get any time together.

They're determined to make the most of each moment, no matter who tries to get in their way.

And did we mention pirates?

For fans of *Dragon Bound* and *Lord's Fall*, passion, playfulness, and adventure abound in this Elder Races novella.

Look for these titles from Thea Harrison

THE ELDER RACES SERIES – FULL LENGTH NOVELS

Published by Berkley

Dragon Bound

Storm's Heart

Serpent's Kiss

Oracle's Moon

Lord's Fall

Kinked

Night's Honor (*September, 2014)

ELDER RACES NOVELLAS

Published by Samhain Publishing

True Colors

Natural Evil

Devil's Gate

Hunter's Season

The Wicked

OTHER WORKS BY THEA HARRISON

Dragos Takes a Holiday

Pia Saves the Day (*June, 2014)

Peanut Goes to School (*July, 2014)

GAME OF SHADOWS SERIES
Published by Berkley

Rising Darkness
Falling Light

ROMANCES UNDER THE NAME AMANDA CARPENTER

E-published by Samhain Publishing
(original publication by Harlequin Mills & Boon)

A Deeper Dimension
The Wall
A Damaged Trust
The Great Escape
Flashback
Rage
Waking Up
Rose-Coloured Love
Reckless
The Gift of Happiness
Caprice
Passage of the Night
Cry Wolf
A Solitary Heart
The Winter King (*July, 2014)

6922384R00044

Printed in Great Britain
by Amazon.co.uk, Ltd.,
Marston Gate.